SUNSHINE CAKE

By September Scott

Illustrated by Simone Scholes

FriesenPress

Suite 300 - 990 Fort St
Victoria, BC, V8V 3K2
Canada

www.friesenpress.com

ISBN
978-1-5255-2805-7 (Hardcover)
978-1-5255-2806-4 (Paperback)
978-1-5255-2807-1 (eBook)

1. JUVENILE FICTION, HEALTH & DAILY LIVING, DAILY ACTIVITIES

Distributed to the trade by The Ingram Book Company

For Ariella, Eliseo and Elliot who inspire my imagination each and every day.

And to the cherubs of Barlad, Romania who have forever changed my life.

As the songbirds chirp their
morning tune

Sunlight warms the treehouse
saying farewell to the moon.

The jumping beans hop "clickity-clack!"

"Wake up, Sunshine Cake!
The morning is back."

Wagging his tail, Pumpernickel jumps to the floor

Then over to the table next to the door.

Inside the treehouse, she sets up the tea

And honeysuckle tart with a hint of glee.

As they excitedly sit and sip from each cup

A recipe is made to lift the world up.

They fill a yellow pouch with a
handful of treasures

A dash of joy and kindness and
sweetness beyond measure.

Ready to roll and spice up the day
Sunshine Cake and Pumpernickel
whisk themselves away.

Two doors down, they abruptly stop

Hey! There's a new kid on the block!

She reaches out her hand
knowing just what to say

"So glad you're here!"
and invites Rev to play.

Skipping along to the beat of their feet

The newfound friends make their way down the street.

Sunshine Cake pauses and
points up to the sky

Look at the beautiful trees,
birds and bees passing by!

Off to the post office to mail a handwritten letter

It's just the thing to help Grandma feel better.

Next, they visit kids sifting through a rough time

"We sing songs and read books
and it doesn't cost a dime!"

After volunteering, they make their way
to the local pound

Where puppies and kittens
are lost, and then found.

On their way home they
stop at Lickety Split

To drop off daisies for Lizzy,
a perfect fit.

Sunshine Cake and Rev had so much to say
As they sat and reminisced
on their extraordinary day.

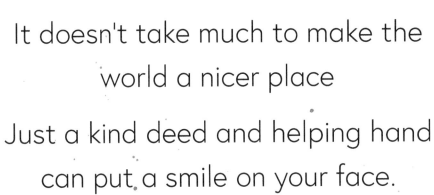

It doesn't take much to make the
world a nicer place

Just a kind deed and helping hand
can put a smile on your face.

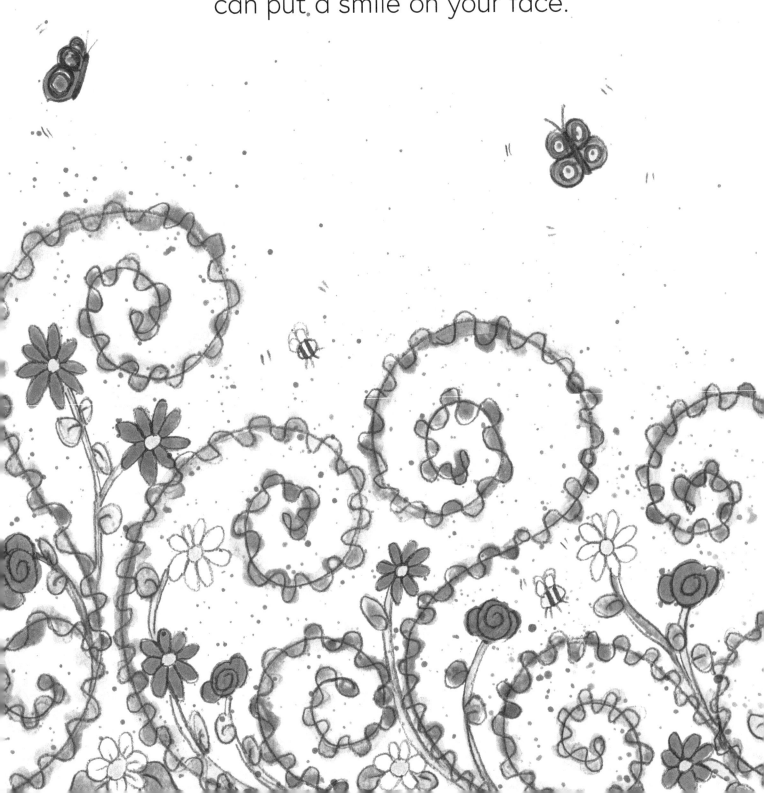

You can whip up joy to make
someone feel more than just fine

Bake up your own adventure and
you, too, can bring sunshine!

Thank you to my dear family
and friends for your infinite love
and support.

And to Stacey for helping me stay
in the sunshine and make this book
become a reality.

photo credit: Lonnie Lippert

September Scott is a storyteller and adventure seeker who has cared for and mentored children the past 20 years. Her passion to promote kindness in our world is the inspiration behind *Sunshine Cake*. September spends much of the year traveling, but calls Austin, Texas home.

Simone Scholes studied art and fashion design in England, which led to her love for painting and illustrating people. Originally from Olde England, Simone now resides in New England with her husband, two sons and two dogs.

www.sunshinecake.com

9 781525 528057